The Argument

Story by Harris Tobias
Illustrated by Sara Iunia Popa

Dedicated to all the beautiful children. May they all get along despite their differences.

There was a time when all birds spoke the same language. They would meet annually in a great convention.

At this meeting they would exchange stories and news and there was good fellowship and good feelings all around. Then one year an argument arose between the pelicans and the ravens as to which bird was the best flyer.

The pelicans demonstrated their trick of catching fish in mid flight.

"Very impressive," said the raven, "but can you do this?" And he proceeded to fly upside down. The argument soon spread to the other birds.

"It is I who fly the best," said the hummingbird, "as I can hover in mid air. I can even fly backwards; and my wings beat faster than the eye can see."

"No, it is I," said the eagle, "With my great wings, I can ride the winds all day without exertion. Besides, I can see a tiny mouse from a thousand yards away."

"I am the best flyer," said the owl. "I can see in the dark and fly without making a sound. Nothing can hear me until it's too late."

"You are all mistaken," said the albatross, "for there are none that can fly as far from land as I. I can be at sea for days and not get lost. Who among you can say as much?"

The condor spread his enormous wings and said that he could stay aloft for an entire day without tiring.

The swallows protested that they flew the farthest.

Not so said the geese who traveled from the arctic to the equator.

"We cranes cross half a world every year", exclaimed the cranes.

The hawks insisted that they were the fastest.

The pigeons and the crows said that they were the most acrobatic.

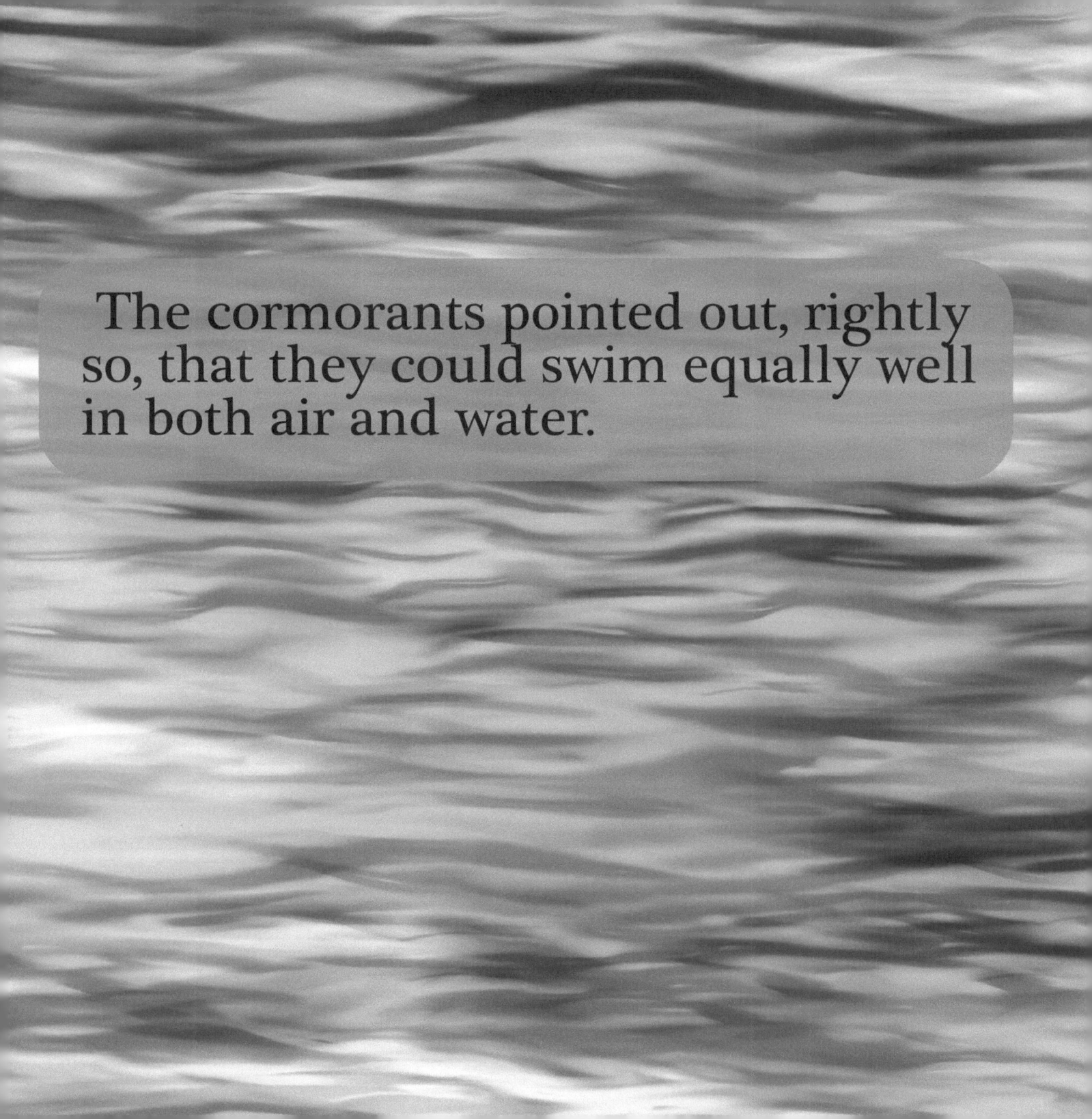

The cormorants pointed out, rightly so, that they could swim equally well in both air and water.

The ducks challenged any bird to land on the water as well as they.

It didn't take long before the argument grew heated and birdie tempers flared. Insults were hurled and feelings were hurt. It didn't take long before the birds from the different delegations refused to speak to one another. The convention broke up in discord and acrimony never to be convened again.

And this is why, to this day, all of the different birds sing different songs and no two kinds of birds speak the same language.

The End

www.ingramcontent.com/pod-product-compliance
Lightning Source LLC
Chambersburg PA
CBHW041012170626
46815CB00003B/268

* 9 7 8 1 9 4 3 3 1 4 2 9 4 *